alien KID

Kristen Otte

Alien Kid

First Print Edition: 2017

Editor: Candace Johnson

Cover Design: Glendon Haddix (Streetlight Graphics)

ISBN: 1546482261

ISBN: 978-1-5464-8226-0

This book is dedicated to the kids who feel like aliens in their school. Hang in there.

ONE

I stepped up to the plate with a slight tremble in my step. Caden held the red ball by his side. He took a big step forward and rolled it at me. I only had a few seconds to decide. *Why did I have to be the first person? The name of the game is kickball, so I have to kick it, right?* I kicked the ball as hard as I could. The ball sailed over Caden's blond head.

"Run!" yelled my classmates.

"Hot Spaghetti!" I shouted as I dashed to the closest base on the left.

Laughter and shouts erupted as I ran, but I didn't stop. When I was within a few steps of the base, I took a flying leap and landed on it. The first baseman on the other team laughed. I smiled ... until I saw the red ball thrown across the field to a different base. My teammates continued to shout, but all the voices and laughter smashed together into a jumble of sounds.

With his foot on the base, Caden caught the red ball.

"Out," he shouted with a big grin.

"Charlie, you're out," Mr. Wells said. He motioned to me, so I jogged to where he stood behind home plate. "You ran to the wrong base. That is third base, not first." I scratched my head.

"That means we run in a counterclockwise direction for this game," I said.

Mr. Wells raised his eyebrows. "I suppose so," he said.

"I thought clockwise was the standard circular direction here."

"Go wait in line with the rest of your team," Mr. Wells said.

I shrugged, confused. I knew I wasn't supposed to use my ability, but I needed answers. I looked at his face and concentrated, but only a few thoughts swirled in Mr. Wells's brain. *What kid doesn't know how to play kickball? What a strange kid!*

I sighed and walked to the end of the line of my teammates. I watched from the sidelines, trying to understand how to play kickball. I didn't want to mess up again and draw more attention on myself. It was enough that I was the new kid at Silver Lake Middle School.

After four more kids kicked the ball, I followed my teammates onto the gym floor to switch roles in the game. When I'd gone to a baseball game with my dad this summer, the teams did the same thing. *That's it! This game is like baseball. Why isn't it called baseball kickers?*

While I waited on the side, my teammates shouted base names and positions to each other as they took their spots. I couldn't remember all the terms in baseball like shortstop, or the rules to the game. Baseball and Kickball were two more games I needed to add to my never-ending list of Earthly things to research. Besides sports and games, I needed to study movies, books, television shows, history, and more. I didn't know how I was going to learn everything in time to fit in here.

I ran to the open space in the back of the gym and waited for the ball. When Mr. Wells blew his whistle to signal the end of the game, the ball hadn't rolled my direction. I jogged to the locker room. Caden was sitting in the front of the locker room on a bench.

"What planet are you from that you don't know how to play kickball?" Caden asked. His bright green eyes stared into mine.

"Jupiter," I said, even though no life could sustain on Jupiter. But life was present on one of Jupiter's moons …

"You think you are funny," Caden said. He took

three steps closer, so I backed up into the wall. He was at least a head taller than me.

"A little bit." I grinned. Caden's smile turned into a frown. "I mean, I want to be funny. I think humor is good for the soul." I had read that once.

"Let's go," Jordan said. "Baker is a weirdo."

"I know you are new to Silver Lake, so I'll let you in on a secret. The sixth-grade boys follow my lead, so don't get in my way."

"I'm not in your way," I said as Caden and Jordan walked past me and out of the locker room, slamming the door behind him. The other guys shook their heads as they passed me to leave the locker room. I had no idea what had just happened, but I knew Caden didn't like me for some reason.

I changed quickly and stepped out of the locker room into the busy hallway of Silver Lake Middle School. I hurried to my locker. Maya Bennett stood at her locker, the one right next to mine. She was in my gym and math classes, but I hadn't heard her speak a word yet. She was tall and skinny, with brown skin and brown eyes, and her black hair was in long, tight twists. More of the kids at this school had the same white skin that I did, so she stuck out a bit. Before I realized it, I was reading her thoughts.

Why do I have the locker next to the new kid? Where did he come from?

"Cleveland," I said without thinking.

She peeked her head out from around the locker.

Oh pug. I did it again. I need to control my ability here.

"Did you just say Cleveland?"

"No," I said and turned away. *Lickity split! I'm really messing things up. It's only the first day, and we're going to have to move.*

"Yes, you did," she said.

"I don't know what you are talking about. I need to get to class." I took my class schedule out of my pocket. Art was next. I turned around and threaded my way through the crowd. But as I hurried away, I realized I was going the wrong way, so I spun around again. The hallway traffic had disappeared, and that wasn't a good sign. I sprinted down the hallway and crossed into the doorway of my art class as the bell rang. The only open seat was in the front row.

I survived the next few classes and lunch without embarrassing myself or causing any trouble. I only had one more class left in the day—history. I hurried around the building and entered the classroom. The teacher was a short, older lady with white hair down to her shoulders.

"Name?" she asked.

"Charlie Baker," I said.

"Front row, front seat." She motioned to the seat in

front of her. I groaned. I didn't know why all the teachers today assigned seats based on our last names but called us by our first names. It didn't make sense to me. Maya, with the last name Bennett, was in the seat behind me.

I turned around and gazed across the faces to see Caden and Jordan in the middle of the classroom. When I tried to focus on their thoughts, I couldn't pick either one out from among the sea of thoughts and voices in the room. I needed more training, but Dad didn't want me to use my ability here. He didn't know that reading the minds of my classmates might be necessary for me to survive middle school on Earth.

Mrs. Roberts strolled to the front of the room, and the voices quieted. I concentrated on her mind. A fat orange-and-white cat entered my mind. *I did it! Wait a second. That can't be right.* I concentrated on her mind again. *Still the cat!* I channeled further to learn the cat's name was Meowser. *Oh, pug.* The bell rang, and her thoughts cleared.

"Today we start to learn the heart of American history. We start with the first settlers to come to the United States. Can anyone tell me who they were?"

A hand shot into the air in the front row three seats to my right.

"Yes, Erin?"

A girl with glasses and dark hair smiled. "The Pilgrims."

"Ahh. That's a common misconception."

What is a misconception?

"The pilgrims arrived not long after this first colony. Anyone else?"

I stared into Mrs. Roberts's eyes and found the answer. I raised my hand.

"Yes, Charlie?"

"Jamestown," I said.

A warm smile broke across her face. "Very good," she said.

Erin turned and looked at me with wide eyes.

"Charlie, do you know when Jamestown was founded?"

"1607," I said. *Maybe school wouldn't be so hard after all.*

"Yes, that is correct. Okay, class. Open your books. We are going to learn more about Jamestown." Mrs. Roberts walked to her desk, grabbed a stack of papers, and handed them to the class. We spent the rest of the time filling out the handout while Mrs. Roberts sat at her desk, probably thinking about her cat. I couldn't tell because once the work was passed out, I focused all my energy on getting it done before class ended.

When the bell rang, I followed my classmates out of the room to our lockers. I filled my backpack with the books I needed, slammed the locker door shut, and turned around. Caden leaned against the gray lockers with his arms crossed.

"So, you're a smart guy?" he said.

"Not really," I stammered.

"You just had to show you were the smartest on the first day of school."

Did he want me to agree with him? Quick. Think.

"Yes," I said.

His face scrunched. He took a step closer so I could feel his stinky-feet breath on my face. The combination of his bad breath and the anger pulsing from him made me look away.

"Nerds aren't welcome in this school," he said. He lunged forward, shoving me into the lockers. My head swung back and hit the locker.

"Ow!" I said. I rubbed the back of my head as he walked away.

Maya approached her locker, entered her combination, and opened it.

"You should stay away from Caden. He's trouble," Maya said. I took a step to the left.

"He's finding me," I said, opening my own locker.

"That's even worse."

"Yeah. I don't know what I did."

"You're new. He did the same thing to me last year when I moved to Silver Lake," Maya said. She shut her locker and flung her backpack over her right shoulder.

"So how did you get him to leave you alone?" I asked.

"You moved here."

I squinted at her. "What?"

"He's got someone new to pick on."

"Oh."

Better you than me.

"What do you mean?" I asked. She squinted at me. *Wait, did she say that? No. That was her thought.*

"I need to go," she said and hurried away. *Lickity split, I did it again.* I sighed and followed the crowd of students out of the building, but I walked home alone. My first day of middle school had not gone well, and I had no idea how to make tomorrow better.

TWO

"How was your first day of middle school?" my father asked as he looked up from his laptop. He was seated at the dining room table. I sighed and then I felt his presence enter my thoughts. Someday I would be able to block him from entering my head without asking, but I doubted I would need to. Secrets were an Earthly thing.

"You need to be more careful," he said.

"I know." I sat on the couch in the living room within eyesight of my father. I heard a clank in the kitchen. My mom was home too.

"We have talked about this. You are not to use your ability on humans. They have no way to fight it."

"I'm not trying to use it all the time. It just happens sometimes." My father nodded. "Honestly, I couldn't believe that I could read Mrs. Robert's mind with everyone in the room."

"That's impressive," my father said. "Your ability is strong already."

"I want you to teach me."

"I will someday."

"Why not now?" I asked.

My mother entered the dining room from the kitchen.

"It's not the right time. We need to blend in the best we can in this town," she said.

"I've been waiting for my ability to manifest for years," I said, "but when it does, I can't really use it. That rains cats and dogs on the parades."

My parents looked to each other and shook their heads.

"I don't think you got that saying right," my mother said. "I think you mean raining on my parade."

"Or it's raining cats and dogs," my dad added.

I squinted at them. "No way. Neither of those make any sense."

My mom and dad sighed in unison.

"They might not make sense to us," my mom said. "But your language use needs some work. We will have to add English back into your training before your incorrect use of weird Earthly sayings gets us discovered!"

"'Boy discovered to be alien by his bad use of

jokes',"I said. We all laughed. My mother turned to face me.

"In all seriousness, you do need to be careful with your ability."

"I know, Mom."

The front door opened. Katie, my nine-year-old sister, stepped inside.

"Hi," she said.

"How was school?" I asked.

"It was great. I made a few friends, and I didn't have to do any work today."

"I'm jealous."

"Why?" she asked.

"Everyone in the school doesn't like me, and it's only been one day."

"The same thing would have happened on our planet," Katie said.

I glared at her. "Not true!"

"School and friendships are more complicated as you get older, no matter where you live," my father said.

"But on Europa, I wouldn't get shoved into a locker for no reason," I said.

"No, but our society on Europa is much different from Earth's. Or rather, it was much different." My dad looked to the floor and sighed. "But we are here now, maybe forever, so we need to adapt."

"What happened, Charlie?" my mother asked, changing the subject away from our former life.

"I got off on the wrong toe with a kid named Caden."

"What?" my mother and sister said in unison. I told them about gym class, history class, and Caden's reactions.

"What if you did something nice for Caden?" she said.

"Got any ideas?" I asked.

"Maybe get him flowers," my dad piped in. "This morning I learned that's a nice thing to do for my wife on Earth. I bet it's the same for friends."

"Flowers. Yeah. I can do that. Where do I get them?"

"Get some from outside."

"Like anywhere?"

"Sure. I don't see why not," my father said.

"Okay." I put on my shoes and walked out the front door. We had some yellow flowers in our front yard, so I pulled two out of the ground. Then I surveyed the yards around us and spotted bright red flowers in the garden two houses down from us. I jogged through the yards to them and grabbed the stem of one.

"Hot Spaghetti!" I yelled. A drop of blue blood bubbled on my finger. I shook my hand until the bleeding stopped. Examining the flower closer, I noticed thorns going up and down the stem. *Forget these.* I turned and saw some white flowers across the street. I skipped to them. This time I didn't grab them right away until I inspected them. When I didn't see any thorns, I pulled a few out of the ground.

The front door opened.

"Hello!" I said and grinned.

"What are you doing?" the older woman asked.

"Your flowers are nice, so I'm taking a few for a friend."

"What? You can't take flowers out of my yard."

"I can't?"

"No!" she yelled. I looked at her face. *Who is this kid?* Then I felt anger beginning to well inside the older woman.

"Sorry," I said.

I dashed down the street toward my house and ran inside. I slammed the door shut, panting. "We have to move," I said.

"What happened now?" my dad asked, but I could feel him search my memories.

"Oh, Charlie, I'm sorry. We all still have a lot to learn about Earth."

"We've been on the planet for a year! And you didn't know that? I don't know what we are doing here."

My father approached me and put his hand on my shoulder.

"Son, we have nowhere else to go right now. We will make it work."

I sighed. "I know. It's just hard."

"I know, son. Let's trim these flowers and put them in water overnight. Since you got them, you should use them tomorrow to help make friends."

I gave my dad the flowers. He took them to the kitchen, filled a glass with water, and placed them in the glass.

My dad was right. We were here for awhile, so I needed to figure out this life. I went upstairs to do some research on the game of kickball.

THREE

With the bundle of flowers in my hand, I shut the car door and waved good-bye to my mother. I followed the crowd of students through the hallways to my locker in the back of the school.

When I arrived at my locker, Maya focused on me and then looked down to the flowers in my hands. Her eyes widened.

"Hey," I said. She didn't respond, so I shoved my coat in the locker and grabbed my math book. With my math book in one hand and the flowers in the other, I walked to class. The classroom only had a few students sitting in their desks, so I took my seat and waited. When I heard Caleb's voice, I turned around to see him enter the room. With two minutes to spare before the first bell, I stood and walked to his desk with the flowers behind my back.

"Hey," I said.

"What do you want?" he asked with a scowl.

"Listen, I think we got off on the wrong finger," I said.

"What?" He squinted his green eyes.

"These are for you." I handed him the flowers. "I'd like to be your friend."

His face turned red as I heard snickers throughout the room. *That is a good sign, right?* Even with all the students in the room, I felt anger seeping from him. *Oh pug. What did I do now?*

The bell rang.

"Please be seated everyone," Mr. Makimoro said. I left Caden's desk and returned to mine. The rush of anger faded as the distance increased between Caden and me.

Mr. Makimoro began his lesson on ratios, but math on Earth was simple compared to what I'd learned on Europa. I glanced over my shoulder at Caden. He shook his head slowly from side to side while he stomped on the flowers with his feet under the desk.

Did I get the wrong kind of flowers? I slumped farther into my seat.

When the class ended, I didn't know whether to approach Caden or leave him alone. Luckily, he was one of the first to leave the class, so I didn't have time to make that decision.

I felt a tap on my shoulder, so I turned to face Maya in the desk behind me.

"Why did you do that?" she asked.

"I thought he'd like them."

"What planet are you from?" she asked. *Lickity split! Does she know my secret?*

"Why are you asking me that?"

"Look, Charlie. I don't know what kids did at your last school in Cleveland, but here you only get flowers for someone you like."

"Isn't that what I did?"

"Man, you really are clueless. Flowers are something boys usually get girls that they like."

"Not friends?"

"No. You get flowers for your girlfriend."

"So now the class thinks I want to date Caden?"

"Maybe." Maya paused. "Do you want to date Caden?"

"No, I just want to be his friend. I was trying to do something nice for him, so he would like me."

"Now he hates you even more. You embarrassed him."

"What do I do?"

"I don't know." I could feel her pity and sadness for me. My parents weren't any better at understanding Earth people than I was. I needed someone to teach me the strings ... or was it ropes? How did that saying go?

"Can you help me?" I asked.

"Help what?"

"Well, life was much different in Cleveland. Can you teach me how to act here?"

"I don't know."

"Please."

"We better get to our next class." She walked out of the classroom.

Mr. Makimoro poked his head in from the hallway. "Charlie, you need to get moving so you aren't late."

I left the room.

———

Avoiding Caden the rest of the day was tricky, especially in the locker room before and after gym class. But when the final bell rang, we hadn't had any more interactions. I went to my locker.

"Are you walking home?" Maya asked. I nodded. "Where do you live?"

"Hunter Woods," I replied.

"C'mon, let's go."

"Together? Wait, does that mean—"

She interrupted me. "Just walk. We need to get out of this school before Caden sees you. Let's go out the back."

She led me down the hallway and through the gym

and out the doors. Teachers were getting into their cars, but we were the only students in sight.

"Why can't we walk out the front?"

She shook her head. "You really are clueless. Caden is mad. He uses his fists if he gets mad."

"Uses his fists to do what?" I asked.

Maya shook her head again. "He wants to beat you up. You need to watch your back."

"I'll be fine. I can feel him coming."

She turned and looked at me, puzzled. "You're weird."

"Thanks," I said.

"That's not a good thing."

"Weird means different, right? Don't people pride themselves on their individuality or differences?"

"Not in middle school," she said.

Oh, pug. I really did need her help.

We walked around the track and then past the baseball field. Trees bordered the field, but I could see the neighborhood through them. As we approached the trees, a narrow dirt path emerged. Maya led the way through the woods until the path ended in someone's backyard. I followed her around the yard to the front of the house. At the sidewalk, I paused.

"Where are we going?" I asked. This street didn't look familiar.

Maya stopped and looked at me.

"We need to talk. You've said some crazy things in

the past two days. If you want me to help you, I need you to be straight with me."

"Straight?"

"Tell me the truth."

"About what?"

"You aren't from Cleveland."

"I lived there for about a year," I said.

Where are you from?

"I can't tell you that."

"Can't tell me what?"

"Where I am from."

"See! That's weird. I never asked you that. How did you know what I was thinking?"

"I guessed," I said. *I did it again. My parents are not going to be happy.*

"It's like you can read my mind. You did it yesterday at my locker."

"I don't know what you're talking about." I started to walk away, then began jogging to distance myself from her. She sprinted to catch up with me. *Gosh, she is fast.*

"That's it!" She stopped. "Oh my gosh. I don't want to help you if you can read my thoughts. I don't want to know who or what you are." She turned away and started walking.

Second day of school and I've already revealed myself to someone.

"No, Maya, wait, please. I really need your help. I

won't read your mind. I am learning to control it better. Please." Maya stopped.

"You promise not to read my mind?"

"I can't promise yet. It's very new to me. But I'll try my best to block your thoughts."

"How can you read minds?"

"Every Jovian can."

"Jovian?"

"It's what people from Jupiter are called."

"You're from Jupiter?"

"Technically, I'm from one of its moons, Europa."

"No way."

"I'm serious. Promise me you won't tell anyone. Not your family, not my family, not your best friend. Can you do that?"

She shrugged. "Okay."

"Promise?"

"I promise."

"Where I come from, we communicate through telepathy. That's how I can read minds." I looked at Maya. She started laughing.

"That's funny. You are weird."

"No, I'm serious."

"Right," she said, shaking her head.

"Will you help me? I need to fit in at Silver Lake."

"I don't know."

"Please. You're my only chance of being able to stay here. Just help me with Caden."

"Fine." We started walking again on the sidewalk. *Why am I helping this guy?* I ignored her thought.

"How can I survive if Caden is out to get me?"

"You need to lay low."

"Lay down on the ground?" She giggled. "What?" I asked.

"Lay down?"

"You said lay low. Isn't that what you meant?"

"Um. No," she said, shaking her head again. "You need to stay away from Caden. You need to not make a scene, and stay quiet in school so he forgets about you."

"Oh. That's it? I can do that."

"Nothing weird. At all."

"Okay. I get it."

"My street is this way. I'll see you tomorrow."

We had arrived at an intersection. I looked up at the signs. *Hunter Woods.* At least I was on my street, but I had no idea which direction to go to find my house. Directions were not one of my natural aptitudes.

"Hasta la vista," I said. I'd heard that once. She chuckled and left.

I walked home deep in thought. Somehow I had to block my parents from what just happened because they'd make us move if they found out Maya knew our secret. I didn't want to move yet. I wanted to give Silver Lake a chance, even if Caden wanted to punch me.

When my house was in sight, I started thinking

about my homework. When I walked into my house, my sister was doing homework in the living room. I heard my dad in the kitchen prepping for dinner, so I shouted hello and went upstairs. I waved to my mother working at her desk in the office, and then went into my room. I started my homework, trying to focus all my thoughts on it, not on Maya or anything that happened that day. It was going to be a long night of focus. Somehow, I couldn't let my parents into my head.

FOUR

Except for dinner, I stayed in my room all night. My parents kept checking on me, but I was watching videos about kickball and baseball, so they didn't ask too many questions. When they finally went to bed, it was close to midnight. I kept myself awake for another half hour with any distraction I could find on the internet, trying to keep Maya out of my mind. At 12:30 a.m., I set my alarm for five o' clock so I'd wake up before my parents.

When the soft buzzing noise woke me, my head felt like a brick had hit it from the lack of sleep and the strain on my brain from trying to keep my parents out of my thoughts. I listened to the silence in the house and worked up the motivation to get out of bed. The wood floor was cold on my bare feet as I walked down the stairs. I grabbed a blanket and the television remote, and I sprawled on the couch. After only a few minutes, my eyes felt heavy. I smacked myself in the face and stood up. I went to the kitchen and dumped four scoops of coffee and some water into the machine, then watched the brown liquid fill my cup. I waited until it finished and then took a big sip.

"Ugh!" I groaned and spit the coffee into the sink. *How do my parents drink this stuff?* Either way, it served my purpose. I was wide awake now. I watched television until I heard my parents stirring. Then I turned off the television, lights, and hurried into the shower to avoid my parents and any questions they might ask.

When I got out of the shower, it was only seven o'clock, but I couldn't stay in the house any longer with my thoughts centered on Maya.

"I need to go to school early today," I said to my father. He was sipping coffee in the kitchen.

"Do you need a ride?" he asked. I shook my head.

"See you later." I left the house quickly and walked at almost a jog down the street. When I was five houses away, I breathed a sigh of relief. The sun was rising, and a pinkish color filled the sky. I didn't know how to keep up not telling my parents. I wasn't made to lie, but I didn't want to cause my parents stress. *Oh pug.*

———

I heard a few teachers in conversation as I entered the

empty halls of Silver Lake Middle School. School didn't start for another forty minutes, so I was the only student wandering the halls.

As I circled the building for the third time, students began to enter the main entrance. I waited in the hallway opposite the front doors, watching for Maya. After ten minutes, I circled back to our lockers. She wasn't there, but I saw Caden's blond, shaggy hair above the crowd farther down the hallway. Maya told me to stay out of his way, so I doubled back to our math class.

Maya wasn't there either, but I sat down anyway. At least in the classroom Caden couldn't shove me into a locker. When the first bell rang, Maya shuffled into her seat behind me. I turned to say hello, but she ignored me. Before I could ask why, the bell rang and Mr. Makimoro started his lesson.

Following Maya's advice to not make a scene, I didn't say a single word during class even though I knew the answers to every math problem. When the bell rang, Maya dashed out of the room before we could talk. *I hope she still wants to be my friend.*

———

The rest of the day was similar to math class, so when the final bell of the day rang, I didn't expect Maya to wait for me. Instead, I waited in the classroom for the hallways to thin.

"Time to go home, Charlie," Mrs. Roberts said. I gave a half smile and left the classroom. The sixth-grade locker bay was empty when I reached it. I tried to remember what homework I had for the day when a voice popped into my head.

There he is. I can't wait to bash his face.

The voice was Caden's. I looked around but didn't see him anywhere. *Peaches and cream! How did I read his thoughts? Where is he?* I scanned the locker bay again and saw a quick movement to my right. They were close, but not in sight. *How did I hear him?* Either way, I needed to get out of the school.

I turned the opposite direction and walked around the corner to my locker. Maya was there. She would know what to do.

"Maya, I'm in trouble," I whispered. "I need your help."

"What?" she said.

"Caden and I think Jordan are around the corner. They're going to follow me, and I don't know what to do."

"I'm sure it's fine. They're probably on their way home by now."

"No, they're not."

"Did you see them?"

"Not exactly"

"Then how do you know?"

"You know," I said with a wink.

"Not this again."

"Can you just tell me a way to sneak out of this school?"

She sighed. "Where are they?" she asked. I pointed to the right.

"Okay. Go left to the seventh-grade locker bay. There is an exit that leads out the back. You'll end up close to the gym, so you can walk home the same route as yesterday past the baseball field through the houses. You remember that?"

"Yes, I think so. Thanks. Where are you going?"

"I have to check on something here."

I closed my locker gently and listened. I could feel Caden's presence still, but I nodded to Maya and took a few steps in the direction of the seventh-grade bay. When I was out of her sight, I jogged through the locker bays until I found the door. With my heart pounding, I pushed open the door and started running. I didn't want to chance anything.

When I reached the path between the trees, I stopped to catch my breath. I doubled over, panting. I looked around and listened. Someone was coming, so I crept off the path into the trees and peeked back at the field behind the school. I breathed a sigh of relief when I saw Maya's black braids through the trees. I stepped back into the path and waved.

"You were right," she said.

"Right?"

"Caden and Jordan were hiding out in the locker bay. They peeked out a few minutes after you left and stormed off when they realized you left."

"They didn't follow you, right?"

"No. They went out the front entrance."

I let out a deep breath.

"So, you aren't lying. You really can read minds?" she asked. I smiled. "Tell me what I'm thinking about right now."

"Are you sure?" She nodded.

I looked into her eyes and focused on her. I was surprised by the effort it took to read her mind compared to what had happened with Caden. "You're thinking about me."

She groaned. "Good point."

"What about now?"

"You're thinking about Chick-fil-A."

"Wow. And now?"

"A pug named Zelda."

Maya laughed. We started walking down the path.

"So, you can you hear everyone's thoughts all the time?" she asked.

"No, it doesn't work like that. I have to focus in on a person. Too many people and I can't separate between all the noise."

"How long have you been able to do this?"

"Since I turned twelve in August."

"And this ability just appeared then?"

"Yes, it manifests in all Jovians on their twelfth birthday."

"Right," she said, slowly nodding her head.

"I am telling the truth. My whole family is from Europa. We can all do it."

"Fine. Then how come you aren't green or have tentacles for arms?"

"That's a stereotype."

"So you live on another planet and look just like us?"

"We live on a moon. But we don't look like humans. Our bodies transformed when we came here."

"Transformed?"

"It's complicated."

Maya raised her eyebrows. "Why should I believe all this?"

"Hold on," I said. I searched the ground around us and saw some thorns. I poked my finger. "Lickity split!"

"What did you say?"

"Lickity split."

"Everyone will know you are weird if you say that in school."

"Oh," I said as I watched the blue blood bubble out of my finger.

"Does this help?" I stuck my bloody finger in her direction.

Her eyes widened. "Is that your blood?"

"Yes," I said. It wasn't exactly blood, but I didn't want to get into anatomy right now.

"Okay. That's weird." She shook her head.

"Can I ask you a question?" I said.

"Shoot."

"Shoot what?" I asked.

"Shoot nothing. It's a saying." I blinked at her. "It means ask me the question," Maya explained.

"Oh pug," I mumbled.

"What did you say?" she asked.

"Why did you ignore me all day?" She looked to the ground.

Without thinking, I went into her head. There was resistance, but I felt feelings of embarrassment and shame.

"You didn't want to be around me."

"HEY! You said you would stay out of my head."

"Sometimes I can't stop myself."

"Really?"

"I swear."

We stopped at the intersection where we split for our houses.

"I'm sorry I ignored you. I know what it's like being the new kid."

"Thanks," I said.

"I'll see you tomorrow," she said. I smiled. She turned to the left for her street.

Maya took three steps before she turned back to face me.

"You know, you should use your mind reading to do good," she said.

"I'm not supposed to use it here. My parents don't want me to bring attention on us."

"Don't tell them."

"It's not that easy."

"But you could do so much good."

"I don't think so."

"Fine. Be boring and lame. I'll see you tomorrow."

"Will you talk to me tomorrow?"

"Yes."

"Promise?"

She nodded. I smiled and turned toward my house. It would be another long night of keeping my parents out of my head. But I had a friend.

FIVE

For the first time all week, I got lucky. When I arrived at my house, my parents were out running errands, so I searched my dad's desk and computer, trying to find anything related to Europa or our ability. I hadn't found anything when the creak of the garage door stopped me. I darted up the stairs, opened my history book, and poured all my energy into learning about the thirteen colonies.

My dad knocked on the door and popped his head into the doorway of my room.

"Good day at school?" he asked.

"Boring, but that's good, I think."

He smiled. "We are going to order pizza for dinner. Any requests?"

"No, I'm good." *Please leave. Please leave.*

He nodded and left the room. I turned my brain to

my homework, trying not to let any rogue thoughts of Maya enter my train of thought.

Pizza is here. The intrusion of my dad into my head caused me to drop my history book on my toe. *Oh pug.*

I'll be down in a minute. Almost done with the homework.

I wrote the last few words to the question and plodded down the stairs thinking about pizza and only pizza.

My family had started eating without me. My mom had her pizza cut into bite-sized pieces while my dad had his cut into four small triangles. They both used the fork to eat the pizza.

"Good thing we are home," I said.

"Why?" my mother asked.

"Nobody on Earth eats pizza with a fork! If we were out, people would know something was up with us."

"Really?" my dad asked. I turned to my sister. She nodded.

"How did we not pick up on that?" my mom said.

"Knows who?" I asked.

"Huh?" my mom and dad asked in unison.

"It's a saying."

"Did you mean to say who knows," my mother asked.

"Isn't that what I said?"

"No," all three said in unison.

"Hot spaghetti!" While my family laughed at my

mistake, I couldn't stop my brain from wandering to thoughts of Maya.

How can I keep this up?

────────

I woke up the next morning to a tap on my shoulder, and a wave of panic swept over me. I opened my eyes to see Katie and feel a headache that was worse than yesterday's.

"It's seven. Time to get up," she said. I nodded and breathed a sigh of relief, but I couldn't be certain what had happened while I was asleep.

After a quick shower, I went downstairs. My mother drank from her coffee cup and was reading the news on her tablet.

"Hey, Sleepy," she said.

"Hey," I said, waiting for the lecture. After waiting a minute, the panic subsided. "Where's Dad?" I asked.

"He left already."

"I need to get to school. Tell him I said good morning."

I grabbed a granola bar from the pantry and smiled as I left the room. When I was a few houses away, I let my mind ease back to normal. The headache faded to the back of my head, but the exhaustion remained.

────────

Once I entered the school, I waded through the crowd to my locker. Maya was fidgeting with her braids at her locker.

"You don't look good," she said.

"It was a long night."

"Why?"

"It's hard to keep my parents away from my thoughts. They can't know that you know," I whispered.

"Maybe it will get easier with practice," she said.

"Not if I don't have anyone to teach me."

"Maybe I can help?"

"Sorry, not with this," I said.

She shook her head. "I think I can figure something out. Meet me on the path after school."

I wanted to tell her it was impossible.

"Oh pug," I said.

"What?"

"I'll be there."

"That's not what you said," she said. "You said something about a pug."

"No, I didn't." I closed my locker. She crossed her arms.

"Maya!" shouted a tall, dark-haired girl across the hallway.

"See you later," she said and caught up with her friend.

I took my math book and slammed the locker shut.

I heard chuckles behind me, but I ignored them and went to class. My eyes felt heavy after I sat down, so I closed my eyes and rested my head on my desk until the ding of the first bell jolted me from my kitten nap.

"Are you okay?" Mr. Makimoro asked.

"Yes. I didn't sleep much last night."

"You kids. Always staying up watching this or that. You need your sleep."

"I wasn't watching ... never mind."

My classmates filed in and took their seats. After the announcements, Mr. Makimoro began his lesson, but exhaustion weighed on me. I pinched myself several times, but I couldn't stop the sleep from overpowering my body. When I woke up again, the bell was ringing.

"Charlie, please come here."

I walked to Mr. Makimoro's desk.

"I will let it slide this time, but fall asleep again and I'll assign you double homework."

"I'm sorry. It won't happen again." I gave him a half smile and left the classroom.

I rotated through pinching myself and falling asleep during the next several classes. I thought lunch and some food would wake me up, but my full stomach had the opposite effect. I fell asleep during English class.

I woke up to a tap on my shoulder.

"Since you can't bother to stay awake, you can go see the principal."

"Oh, pug," I mumbled. My English teacher, Mrs. Felder, glared at me and handed me a pink slip. The combination of her giant, round belly and her glare gave me a chill. I stood and shuffled to the door.

"Charlie, you will need to take your books with you."

I backtracked to grab my books before entering the empty hallway. I hurried to the principal's office, wondering how he would help my exhaustion. When I arrived at the office, the door was open. A lady with glasses and dark shoulder-length hair was sitting behind a desk and typing.

"Hello," she said with a smile. "What can I do for you?"

"I was sent to the principal's office." I smiled back at her.

"Let me see that." She pointed to the pink slip. I handed it to her.

"Okay. Have a seat." With the pink slip in her hand, she walked into an office behind her. A few minutes later, a very large man with a black mustache and beard stepped into the room.

"Mr. Baker, come in."

I looked around. "Is my Dad here?"

He chuckled. "No. I meant you, Charlie, you come

on in. I like to be formal sometimes. It's part of my charm."

"You can do magic?"

"Trying to be funny, I see. Get in here." He motioned to the doorway. I scampered up and walked into his office. I sat in the chair in front of the large wooden desk. His black swivel chair creaked with the weight as he sat down.

"Why were you sleeping in class?" he asked. He stared into my eyes.

I was in his head. *Another kid sleeping in class. Who cares? He's not causing any trouble. I'd probably have slept through English class, too.*

"Well? Why were you sleeping?"

I blinked a few times. "I didn't mean to. I couldn't sleep last night, and I've been tired all day."

Me too, kid. "Couldn't sleep? Or didn't want to sleep?"

"I wasn't feeling well."

Yeah. Right. He glanced at the clock.

"Since it's the first week, I'll let it slide. But if this becomes a problem, I'll have to take further action, including calling your parents."

"Lickity split. That's not good."

"No, it's not, son." I looked up at him and tuned in, but his mind was blank. *Weird.*

"You can wait in the office until the bell rings," he said. Then his mind went blank again.

How come you aren't thinking about anything?

"Go on, go."

I stood and took the eight steps out of his office and back to the waiting room. The lady at the desk smiled at me. I leaned back in the chair and rested my head against the wall. I didn't know what was the right thing to do. Maybe I needed to tell my parents about Maya.

SIX

A few students walked in front of me through the gym to the back exit of the school. I followed them out the door and into the field. *I guess the path through the woods isn't a secret.* With gray clouds moving overhead, I picked up my pace so I didn't get stuck walking in the rain. I caught up to the guy and girl in front of me. When they turned around and looked at me, I could tell they were eighth graders. They said something to each other before they turned back around, but I couldn't make out the words. A few minutes later, they stopped and spun to face me.

"Hey!" said the tall boy with long, wavy brown hair. The girl's hair was pulled back into ... what was that called? A horsetail?

"Hello!"

"Why are you following us?" I felt suspicion in his thoughts.

"I'm just walking home. I live in the neighborhood back there. Well sort of."

"Sort of?"

"It's not that street, but close to it. I'm meeting a friend on the path."

"Wait, isn't that the kid that gave Caden flowers?" whispered the girl.

Lickity split!

"I need to go so I'll meet my friend in time." I slung my backpack over both arms and sprinted past them as the boy said, "What a weird kid."

With my short legs and poor coordination, I stumbled six times during the run to the path. I stopped at the entrance of the path and doubled over to catch my breath.

"You sure like to make an entrance."

"Hot spaghetti!" I shouted as I jumped a foot in the air. "What did you do that for?" I asked Maya, who stood several feet in front of me on the path.

"Do what?"

"Scare the Mars out of me!"

"Sorry. Why are you running?"

"To avoid conflict." I pointed to the two walking in the field. "They asked if I was the one that gave Caden flowers."

"What did you say?"

"Nothing. I ran."

Maya chuckled. "You are not helping your case."

"My case of what?"

"You need to not be the center of attention."

"I know. That's why I ran."

"But running made you stand out more."

"It did?"

She sighed. I didn't have to read her mind to know that she wasn't feeling great about hanging out with me. We started walking on the path.

"What's your idea?" I asked.

"Are you going to help people?" she asked.

"I can't help anyone if I don't find a way to hide you from my parents."

"Yeah. But I don't want to regret this. Promise me that you will use your ability to help people."

"I'll try."

"Pinky swear." She stopped and reached her hand out.

"What is a pinky swear?"

"A promise you can't break." She paused. "If you break it, your pinky will fall off."

"No way!"

"Yep." She smiled. "You have to pinky swear you will only read minds to help people."

I stretched out my hand. We hooked our pinkies together and wiggled them.

And she thinks that I am weird! "What's your idea?" I asked again.

"You need to tell me everything about how you can read minds."

I started talking. I told her everything I knew about our ability. The two main facts were that it's easier to read minds when I am close to someone and alone with him or her, and that the difficulty increases with distance and more people.

She asked about how I survived the past few days at home.

"Luck and focus. But I can't sustain those. It exhausts me."

"Essentially you need to put the memory of me in the back of your mind. It seems that your ability works best with fresh thoughts and recent memories." I nodded. She continued, "After school, or after seeing me, you need to forget about the day until you leave the next morning."

"I can't just forget."

"I know. But you can stack a bunch of new thoughts and memories over the school day."

"That's what I was doing, and it was exhausting."

"Yes, but not to the level that I'm thinking." She explained her idea.

It was worth a try.

———

When Maya turned for her house, I started on her plan—a new after-school routine. My first stop was the library, which was two blocks away. My legs were dragging, but if this worked, maybe I would get some rest tonight.

I entered the library and found an empty table to do my homework. After finishing my homework, I picked out the first book in the Harry Potter series. Maya said it was a must-read for every kid on Earth. I set a timer on my watch, and twenty minutes later I was surprised that I didn't want to stop reading. I wrote down my page number in my assignment book and put it back on the shelf. Apparently, I could take the book home if I had a card, but I needed my parents for that.

The next stop was the park a few blocks down the street. The clouds had passed, and the sun was out. I didn't understand Earth's weather because one minute it rained and the next it was sunny or snowing! I walked past a playground full of young kids laughing and shouting and another group of what looked like high school kids playing with a flying disc. I walked until I saw a basketball court. The kids—all boys except for one girl—were maybe my age or a little older. I thought, *This might be the best opportunity*, but as with most Earth games, I didn't know how to play.

I walked up to the court during a stop in the game

and asked to play. They agreed without hesitation. I was the shortest kid on the court, but that didn't bother them. They put me on a team and told me they played to eleven. I had no idea what that meant.

After the first time my team had the ball, I knew I had to read minds to figure out what to do. I didn't think Maya would approve, but it was the only way I could play this game. I focused on the boy who said I could join in. With the number of kids and the movement, I couldn't stay focused on him, but I got enough bits and pieces to learn a few things. I needed to stay out of the way when someone on my team was moving toward the basket with the ball. The opposite was true when the other team had the ball. Those two bits helped me survive the game without getting kicked off the court even though I was the reason my team lost.

I looked at my watch. It was close to five. Time to go.

"Thanks for letting me play. I know I'm not real good, but it's fun. Can I come back tomorrow?" A few of the guys looked to the brown-skinned kid with very short black hair. I knew his name was Blake. He was much taller than me, but skinny like me. But he had a toughness to him that my scraggly alien self did not have.

"Okay. You'll get better the more you play," Blake said.

"Thanks. See you guys tomorrow."

I needed to be home soon for dinner, so I walked home instead of doing the last thing on Maya's list. The library and basketball had already given me a bunch of new memories. I'd know soon if her plan would work.

My family was gathered around the table when I walked through the front door.

"There you are," my mother said.

"I had some things to do after school," I said. The memories of the library and park flashed in the front of my brain.

"It's great that you like a game. That will really help you fit in at Silver Lake. I hear that games, or rather sports, are important here," my mother said.

"Is there any risk of you getting hurt while playing?" my dad asked.

"I don't think so. Nobody got hurt today."

"Okay, but if that changes, you need to stop playing. We can't have injuries."

"Okay. What's for dinner?"

"Your dad is trying to make some chicken and something."

"Lickity split!"

"I heard that," he said. I laughed.

Dinner was surprisingly tasty. Maybe my dad was learning the art of Earth cooking. Or maybe he got lucky. Even after a year, we were still adjusting to our earthly bodies and taste buds.

Even with the new memories, my evening was tense because I didn't want to accidentally think about Maya, which made me think of her. It was a constant cycle, but my exhaustion took over by nine o'clock. I couldn't stay awake any longer, so I fell asleep and hoped Harry Potter and basketball were enough.

SEVEN

When my alarm buzzed, the headache of the past two days was gone but I hesitated to get out of bed. Maya had entered my dreams during the night. Before I went downstairs, I showered to clear my head and think about the day ahead.

"Good morning," I said, sitting at the table. My mother smiled and passed me a plate of pancakes.

"How did you sleep?" she asked.

"Like a pebble," I said. She laughed.

"I don't think you got that right."

"You always say that."

"I'm right most of the time."

"I don't know about that. Where's Dad?"

"He's out running a few errands."

"This early?"

She nodded.

My little sister wandered into the kitchen. She slumped into a chair, eyes glazed over.

"What's wrong with you?" I asked.

"I was up watching *Dancing with the Stars* with Mom."

"Weird."

"No, it's amazing," Katie said.

"It's a fascinating culture study of this planet," my mother added.

I'll have to ask Maya about that. Oh pug. I'm thinking about Maya.

"I need to get to school! 'Bye!" I shoved the rest of the pancake in my mouth and rushed out the door.

That was close.

Maya was waiting for me at the locker. Maybe she wasn't waiting for me exactly, but she was at her locker.

"You made it," Maya said.

"Made what?"

"You're at school."

"Yes, I am. But what did I make?"

"You really need a better grasp of English."

"I think I'm pretty good at this language."

Maya shook her head side to side. "Did it work?" she asked.

"I think so."

"You think?"

"I'm pretty sure. I got some sleep, and my parents didn't ask about you. At least not yet."

"That's great."

"Yeah," I mumbled.

"What's wrong?"

"I don't like lying to my parents."

"It's for a good reason."

"Even if it's for a good reason, it's still lying," I said.

"Yeah. I don't like lying to my parents either. What if you just told them about me?"

"Then our family moves."

"But I'm not going to tell anyone else."

"We don't know that."

Maya let out a deep sigh and shook her head.

The bell rang.

"Come on, let's go to class," she said.

———

As I walked to gym class, a bad feeling swept through me. Caden and I hadn't talked since the flowers, and I worried about what he would do next. I paused at the locker room door and took a deep breath to summon all my Jovian courage. When I opened the door, Caden's back was to me, so I hurried past that locker bay to the next. I changed into my gym clothes, put my school clothes in the locker, and shut it. I heard Caden and Jordan talking, so I crept around the locker bay, but they weren't close so I turned the corner and went out the door. I smiled and joined my class. *Maybe I am worried for no reason.*

The gym was set up for another game of kickball. I stood behind home plate, close to Mr. Wells, until I saw Maya emerge from the door of the girls' locker room with a few of her friends. I started to say hello, but the noise of the boys' locker room door slamming drew my attention. I turned to see Caden and Jordan laughing. I tried to read their thoughts, but they were too far away.

Mr. Wells blew his whistle and gathered the class. He split the class into teams, and by a dumb stroke of luck I wasn't on Caden's and Jordan's team. I ran to my spot in right field and stayed out of the way except for one kick that flew over my head. I chased it down, but my classmates laughed when I threw it. I heard someone shout something about a granny. *Doesn't that mean Grandma? I don't see any old people around.*

When gym class ended, I waited an extra minute in the gym. *I'd rather be late to my next class than have a run in with Caden.*

"You need to get changed and go to your next class," Mr. Wells said.

"I know."

"Then do it."

I groaned and went to the locker room. I heard Caden's voice as I opened the door. He was talking about a girl.

"Last year, she was nothing special. I don't know what happened over the summer, but she looks good." I wondered who the girl was that he mentioned. I walked around the corner to my locker and opened it, but my clothes were gone. I turned to Jake, who was sitting on the bench next to me.

"Have you seen my clothes?"

"I'm sorry."

"Sorry?"

"Caden," he whispered.

I crept around the locker room. I couldn't read Caden's mind without getting too close to him, so I took a step into his view across the room from him.

"Charlie, why haven't you changed yet?" Caden asked with a snicker.

"Where are my clothes?"

"They needed a wash to get your stink off," Caden said. Jordan laughed.

I stormed past them to the sinks, but my clothes weren't anywhere. The laughter got louder as I opened the first bathroom stall door to an empty toilet. I closed the door and checked the second to see my jeans and red T-shirt floating on the top of the water. *Gross.* I shut the stall door, leaving my clothes swirling in the toilet. I stormed past Jordan and Caden, who were doubled over with laughter, and left the locker room.

"Mr. Wells, I need to call my parents. I need clothes," I said.

He turned his attention to me. "Why?"

"Someone put my clothes in the toilet."

"Your gym clothes are fine for the day. Go to your next class."

Annoyed, I focused in on his eyes. *A little prank never hurt anyone,* he was thinking.

"Why isn't anyone on my side?" I mumbled as I left the gym. I went straight to my locker.

"Why are you in your gym clothes?" Maya asked.

"Caden put my clothes in the toilet."

"I'm so sorry," she said with a frown. The sympathy was genuine.

I felt a new feeling inside of me–anger—and this anger was growing and was all directed at Caden. I knew gym clothes weren't that big of a deal, but I wanted this feud with Caden to end. *Why can't he let it all go?* If only I could go back and start this week of school over. I couldn't do that, but maybe I needed to use my ability to my advantage.

"What if I got him back somehow?" I asked.

"I don't think that's a good idea."

"You were the one who said to use my ability for good."

"Yeah, but ... that's not what I meant."

"Caden is a jerk!"

"I know."

"Then let's make a plan after school today. Let's get him back so he'll stop harassing us forever!"

"I don't think it's a good idea," she said, shaking her head.

"We'll talk after school. Meet here?"

"Fine," she said.

I trudged to the next class.

EIGHT

I couldn't get Caden out of my head for the rest of the day. The more I thought about him and all that had happened, the angrier I got. When the final bell rang, I was determined to do something—but I didn't know what to do. I wanted him to leave me alone, but I didn't know how to do that without looking like more of a weirdo.

Maya and I met at our lockers and walked out the back of the school. I shielded my eyes as I walked into the bright sunshine.

"I need to do something," I told her.

"Like what?" she asked.

"Something to embarrass him so he'll leave me alone."

"I don't think that's a good idea, Charlie. You'll just start a feud that will never end."

"The feud already started."

She shook her head. She didn't want to help me, so I searched my mind to find something I could use against Caden. I knew he was a jerk who was good at sports. Neither of those were helpful, but then I remembered his conversation with Jordan in the locker room.

"Hot spaghetti!"

"You say weird things."

"Maya, I know what to do," I said to her as we walked out of the school. "Caden was thinking about a girl that he likes today in the locker room. I will figure out who it is and make sure that he doesn't have a chance with her."

She stopped walking and looked at me. "This is not what I meant about using your ability for good. If you do this, you're no better than him."

"But he deserves it. He's not a good guy."

"I know. But Charlie, don't do this. Just leave it alone."

"I don't know, Maya." We stopped at the intersection. "I need to go so I can finish homework in time to play basketball."

"Wait, you are playing basketball?" she asked with a chuckle.

"Yeah, it was the only game happening at the park that worked for me to play. I'm surprised the guys said I could come back today."

"Were you that bad?"

"Definitely."

She laughed again.

"Maya, do you think I'll make it through the weekend lying to my parents?"

"You'll be fine, Charlie. Just don't do anything stupid with Caden. He'll forget about you eventually."

"Thanks, Maya, but I don't know if I can do that if he keeps messing with me."

I waved to Maya and forged ahead through my new afternoon routine. Without any distractions at the library, I finished my homework quickly, but I lost track of time reading Harry Potter and then had to hurry to the park.

When I arrived, the guys were still playing. They waved me over to them, and I jumped into their game. The teams were different today, and as the game went on, I realized why. They rearranged teams to even them out with me playing.

I managed to learn a little more about basketball by focusing my ability on one player, Blake, since he seemed to be the one running the game. After you passed the ball, the best thing was to run to the hoop. One time I got a pass back and made a shot, but I also tripped over my own feet on the other end, letting the guy go right past me and score. My team lost again, but it was close.

"Thanks for letting me play again. Tomorrow?" They nodded.

When I arrived home, my parents had dinner on the table.

"There you are. Eat some food, then we are heading to the football game," my father said.

"What football game?" I said.

"Silver Lake High School game," he replied.

"Why?"

"Because if we want to make this our home permanently, we need to get out. Katie said a lot of the kids in her school go to the game with their families."

"Okay." *I wonder if Maya will be there.*

My dad jumped into my head.

Lickity split.

You like her.

My face felt like it was on fire.

"What is happening?" I asked.

"I think you are blushing," my dad said.

"It's perfectly natural to start feeling affection toward another person at this age, even on Earth," he said.

"We are just friends."

He raised his eyebrows, but I felt his presence leave my mind. I breathed a sigh of relief.

"I need to go change." I hurried up the stairs and into my room and shut the door. I collapsed on my bed, face-first into my pillow. *Hot spaghetti. That was a close one.*

———

People of all ages streamed into the football stadium. I recognized a few students from my school, and Katie waved to some of her classmates. The evening air was warm, and the sun was setting on the horizon. We walked up the bleachers until my dad waved to a woman who was probably a little older than my parents. We sat next to her, and my father struck up a conversation.

"Does Dad know her?" I asked my mother.

"Yes, I think they met at yoga class."

"Yoga class? What is that?"

"Some Earth exercise that involves contorting your body."

"Why would he do that? Why would anyone do that?" I asked.

My mom shrugged. "You'll have to ask him."

A few families filled the rows around us. I was trapped by my parents on one side and some strangers on the other side. I didn't like being in the center of all these people with all their thoughts and voices. I couldn't read anyone's mind, and the amount of people created a buzz in my head.

We watched the players line up on the field.

A loud buzzer sounded and both my parents darted into a standing position. I shook my head.

"It signals the start of the game," I said to them. Then, a whistle blew, and a swarm of Silver Lake players in white jerseys ran in the direction of the football. They smashed into the other team, but I'm not sure where the ball ended up. Football was another sport that I didn't understand. I knew it involved guys running into each other and tackling, but I hadn't figured out the scoring part yet.

The people around us stood and cheered, so my dad did the same. *Oh, pug. I hate when he does this.* Sometimes he copied the actions of the people around him to fit in. I thought it made him look silly and stand out even more. I needed to get away from him before he made a scene.

"Dad, can I get a snack?" I asked.

"We aren't leaving."

"No, you can get a snack from the concession stand."

"Concession stand? Is that where the team that loses goes?"

"It's where they sell snacks."

"Then why is it called a concession stand?"

"I don't know, Dad. But I'd like some popcorn. Can you give me a few dollars?"

"They have popcorn here?" he asked with wide open eyes. I nodded.

"Get as much popcorn as you can with this," he said. He opened his wallet and gave me a twenty-dollar bill.

"Peaches and cream!" I said.

I bounded down the bleachers and circled around the stadium to the concession stand. I waved to a few familiar faces from my classes, but they didn't acknowledge me. I kept walking and got in line.

"I'll take two pieces of pizza and a soda." I looked to the front of line to see Caden hand a five-dollar bill to the man working the cash register; Jordan stood next to him. *Lickity Split.* I ducked out of line and hid on the other side of the concession stand. The sound of Caden and Jordan's laughter grew louder, so I pressed my body against the building to keep out of sight. They walked right past and didn't notice me hovering next to the building. When they were out of sight, I stepped back into line. I looked at the menu and did some quick math.

"Eight popcorns and a hot cocoa." The man squinted at me.

"Do you have someone with you?"

"My family is here."

"Okay. Seventeen dollars." I handed him the twenty.

He gave me the change and walked behind him. He grabbed a small white cup and filled it with a brown substance, then handed it to me.

"What's this?"

"Hot cocoa. You said one hot cocoa."

"I did. But isn't hot cocoa a bar of spicy chocolate?"

He looked confused. "No. It's a hot drink that's flavored with chocolate."

"Lickity split," I mumbled.

He turned around and began placing the boxes of popcorn on the counter.

Oh pug, how am I going to carry all of these boxes?

"Do you have a bag? Or box?"

"I think so." He returned with a cardboard box. I loaded the popcorn in the box, but I couldn't carry that and the hot cocoa. *What was this hot cocoa?* I took a sip.

"Blah." I spit it out on the ground.

"What is your problem, kid?" A big, burly teenager with a beard asked. He was next in line.

"Nothing." I left the hot cocoa on the counter and tried to see above the big box while I walked. Popcorn was my absolute favorite Earth food, but I hadn't thought this through. I put the box down on the edge of the walkway. I grabbed the first box and started eating, watching the stream of people moving in both directions around the stadium.

I glanced at the scoreboard to see we were losing, but I didn't know why the timer was counting down. *I really need to learn more about all this stuff.* I opened my mouth and dumped the salty, delicious popcorn into my mouth. Once I started eating popcorn, I never wanted to stop. The next three boxes were gone in a few minutes. I cradled the four remaining boxes in my arms and headed through the throng of people to the bleachers. At the stairs, I felt a tap on my shoulder. I turned to see Maya smiling at me.

"Four boxes?"

"For my family," I said with a smile.

"Do you need some help carrying them?"

"Sure." She took two boxes, and I led her up to the bleachers. We were two rows away when I realized we were making a huge mistake.

"Lickity split! You have to go. You can't meet my family. They will know."

"The stadium is packed. Doesn't that make it hard for them to read you?"

"That makes it hard for me, not them. We're family, and they are trained. Here, stack those boxes on top of mine." Maya pursed her lips, but she put the boxes on mine.

"Fine," she mumbled and walked down the bleachers, away from me. I breathed a sigh of relief as I took the last few steps to my family.

"Popcorn! Yes!" Katie said. I handed everyone in my family a box and my dad the change.

"You ate a few more boxes, didn't you?"

"Four," I said with a big grin. He laughed.

"That was Maya, wasn't it?" I nodded. "Why didn't you want us to meet her?"

"I don't want to know how she feels about me. You would know in an instant."

"You don't?" my dad asked.

I shook my head and tried to focus on the game. "I'm staying out of her head, taking your advice. I want to be like any other Silver Lake middle school kid."

"Good. I'm really happy that you are fitting in here." He looked at me.

"I'm trying," I said. *That is the truth.* I turned to the game and focused on the brown thing flying through the air in case my dad entered my head. At least, I was learning my ability, even if it was trial by water. Or was that saying trial by fire?

NINE

I woke up Saturday morning to the sunlight streaming through the window. I hurried down the stairs and walked outside in my pajamas to the contrast of warm sunlight and cool air, which meant today would be a perfect day to spend at the park.

My family was scattered through the house. Katie was watching television with my mom in the living room, while my dad was reading, most likely catching up on the news. I said hello and then popped a bag of popcorn in the microwave and went back upstairs. I spent an hour or two learning about football. Apparently American football was different than football everywhere else in the world. Football in the rest of the world is the game called soccer here in the United States. It was confusing.

I ate lunch with my family and then left for the

park. The guys were there and already practicing. I played three games of basketball before we took a break. I couldn't feel my legs by the time we stopped. We all sprawled across the court, looking at the sky.

"Dude, you didn't even break a sweat!" Malik said.

"I don't sweat much," I said. *Or at all.*

"Lucky," Blake said, rising to his feet. "We better get going." He signaled to Malik.

"Will you guys be here tomorrow?"

"If the weather is good," Blake said.

I limped over to the other side of the park and lay in the grass. When I opened my eyes, I felt something crawling on my face.

"Hot spaghetti!" I shouted.

I jumped to my feet and slapped the creepy-crawly thing off my face. I heard laughter and turned to see a boy about Katie's age watching me and cracking up. He sat on a blanket eating a sandwich with his parents.

I looked at the sun and knew that I had about an hour before my parents expected me home. My legs felt like jelly, but I walked toward the basketball court, expecting it to be empty. I heard the rattle of the ball hitting the rim and the pound of the ball bouncing, but I couldn't see through the trees.

I circled around the trees and then saw Caden and Jordan shooting on one end with another guy I recognized from school.

How does this keep happening? Why do I always run into them?

On the other side of the court, Blake and Malik were shooting. Blake waved.

"You still here?" he asked.

"I'm on my way home. I thought you left," I said.

"We grabbed some food and decided to come back. Not many days left to play outside before fall comes." He smiled. He passed the ball to me.

"Charlie Baker. You play basketball? This has to be funny," Caden said across the court. Jordan snickered.

"You don't have to take that from him," Blake whispered.

"He can beat the living night-light out of me."

"What did you say?"

"He can beat the living night-light out of me."

"Do you mean daylight?"

"Maybe," I said. "Caden shoved me into a locker and threw my clothes in a toilet. I don't know how to get him back without getting my nose broken."

"The guy is a jerk."

"Do you know him?" I asked.

"Only from playing ball against him," Blake said as he turned toward Caden and Jordan. "You guys up for a quick game of three-on-three?" he shouted.

"No," I said. "I'm so tired."

"I've got you."

"Is he playing?" Caden pointed to me. Blake nodded.

"Yeah. Winner buys ice cream." Caden sneered.

"Sure," Blake said.

I sighed, but I lined up at half court with Malik and Blake.

"You losers can have the ball. Play to seven," Caden said.

Blake took the ball, and the game started.

I was shoved and pushed every moment that I didn't have the ball, which was most of the game. Somehow, I fell into a rhythm and didn't play terribly. I scored a basket, stayed out of the way, and even stole the ball a few times because I read exactly where Caden would pass the ball. We won by two.

After the game, Malik, Blake, and I walked out of the park together. Caden was so mad that he stormed off the court and didn't buy us ice cream. I didn't mind. I'd rather have popcorn anyway.

"I can't believe we won. Too bad you two don't go to Silver Lake. Nobody would believe me if I told them I beat Caden at something."

"At least you know the truth, and that's what matters," Malik said.

"Yeah. You two are really good at basketball. Thanks for letting me tag along."

"No problem. We're always up for a game." They smiled and waved as they left the park. I rested for a few minutes, then I walked home in the fading afternoon sun.

———

The skies opened up with rain on Sunday. I buried myself in reading Harry Potter at the library. I finished the first book and moved on to the second. Maya told me to read all seven books, but once I saw the thickness of some of them I wondered if I could. I had never read a book that big before, but the story had hooked me.

Homework kept my family out of my head on Sunday evening. When I went to bed, I felt confident that Maya's plan was working. If I could keep this up, we could stay in Silver Lake and my parents wouldn't find out about Maya.

When I arrived at school early Monday morning, I dropped my coat off at my locker. With my math book in hand, I searched the halls for Caden. I found him alone at his locker. Staying out of sight, I hung back behind the locker bay next to his. I closed my eyes, leaned against the lockers, and focused.

Peaches and cream! I was in his head! He was thinking about what books to bring to class. Then, an image flashed in his memory of his dad yelling, but that quickly left his mind. Nothing about a girl.

"What are you doing?" Jordan asked. I opened my eyes. He was standing two feet in front of me.

"Nothing." I started to move away, but he stepped in my path.

"I asked you a question."

"I can't stand in the hallway?"

"Not over here."

"Okay." I went the opposite direction.

"Loser," he said under his breath. I circled the hallway back to Caden's locker. I peeked around the bay again to see Jordan and Caden talking. With more students roaming the hallways, they didn't notice me. I backed up behind the locker, closed my eyes, and concentrated on Caden's location. A few different voices entered my head. None were Caden.

I opened my eyes and peeked around the corner of the locker again. Caden and Jordan were laughing. I zeroed in on Caden and found his thoughts. After a few minutes of football replays in his head, I felt the excitement of something else. He was thinking of the girl. I focused, and Maya's image fluttered into my head.

Maya? Caden likes Maya! Oh pug. I left Caden's mind and sighed.

"What are you still doing here?" Jordan asked. I jolted out of my head and opened my eyes. Caden and Jordan, their arms crossed, stood in front of me.

"Lickity split!" I darted the opposite direction,

weaving in and out of students to escape Caden and Jordan. When I reached the seventh-grade hallway, I stopped running. Sprinting in the hallway was going to help me keep my reputation as the weird kid for another week. At least I hadn't been shoved into a locker or thrown in a toilet. *Can I fit in a toilet?* I didn't want to find out.

With my eyes and brain on alert, I went back to the sixth-grade hallway. I didn't see them anywhere, so I went to math class. Mr. Makimoro was typing at his desk while I took my seat. Maya walked in a few minutes later.

"Hey," she said. "How was your weekend?"

"It was good," I said.

"No issues?" she said under her breath.

"Nope."

I looked at her. Caden liked her. *What do I do now?*

TEN

The next week was a blur with homework and basketball. Since it was the second week of school, the teachers ramped up the workload. Plus, we had dry weather all week, so I spent the afternoons at the basketball court. Before I realized it, the week was almost over. I had walked home with Maya every day, but I still hadn't told her that Caden liked her.

On the way to school on Friday, I mulled over how to tell Maya about Caden. I couldn't wait any longer. She deserved to know, and I didn't want to hide anything from her. I'd tell her on the way home today.

The teacher let us out of science class a minute after the bell. I rushed to the gym, but I saw Caden and Jordan enter the locker room ahead of me. I ducked inside the door and walked to the back lockers before they noticed me. I changed, locked my clothes up, and hurried onto the gym floor.

Mr. Wells had a football in his hands. *This isn't good.* The rest of the class filtered in over the next few minutes. With everyone present, Mr. Wells explained the rules to play flag football. But he didn't really explain how to play football, only how to remove one of the flags or bandannas from an opposing player. *I guess the bandannas replace tackling. That's a plus.*

When he split us into teams, I ended up on the same team as Caden. Of course, he designated himself the quarterback, the most important player on the team. I had learned about the quarterback from my research the other day, but I was very sketchy on how this game worked. I didn't know when he would throw the ball or if he would throw the ball to me.

I lined up with the rest of my team. When Caden got the ball, I sprinted ahead, turned, and looked at Caden. He was running with the ball, so I stopped. His bandanna was ripped out of his pocket a few feet from where he started. I couldn't tell if that was a good thing or bad thing.

This scene repeated a few more times before the other team got the ball. I'm not sure how or why that happened, but it did. This time, I hung back a little bit until Maya caught a short pass and started sprinting past all the guys. I heard the voices yelling for me to stop her, but she was my friend. I got out of her way, and she dashed past me all the way to the goal.

"What are you doing, loser?" Caden shouted. "Why didn't you stop her? You let her score on purpose!"

"I'm sorry," I mumbled. *I did the wrong thing. Again.*

When we got the ball back, I repeated my pattern of running forward. The other team stopped paying attention to me because they knew Caden would never give me the ball. When I realized that was happening, I stopped running. Instead, I walked ahead about ten steps and waited for the play to end. The third time I didn't even turn to see what Caden was doing. I smiled at Maya and then turned to face Caden when I saw the brown ball flying fast at me.

BONK! I crumpled to the ground, grabbing my face. I felt blood beginning to seep from my nose. *Oh pug!* I covered my nose and dashed to the locker room. The blue blood started to gush into my hand. I ran into the shower and ducked my head under the water. The blue blood swirled down the drain until I felt my nose tighten. I turned the water off and crept around the corner to make sure I was still alone. I took a deep breath when I didn't see anybody. I turned back to face the mirror, looking for blue on me or my shirt. Somehow, the shirt was clean. Finally, I had a stroke of good luck. I took a seat on the bench in the locker room.

"Charlie?" Mr. Wells called.

"Yeah."

"Are you okay?"

"I'm fine. My nose was bleeding, but it stopped."

"Oh good. You can go ahead and change. We only have ten minutes left."

"Thanks." I changed into my street clothes and left the locker room. When I returned to the gym, Caden winked at me.

Peaches and cream! He did it on purpose!

I had to do something.

———

"Maya, I have to do something. You saw gym class today. He threw a football at me!"

"What are you going to do?"

"Something that will embarrass him and get him to leave me alone."

"What is that?"

"I don't know yet. I need your help."

We paused in the middle of the path.

"No. I won't help with this. I already told you why."

She walked ahead. I groaned and hurried to catch back up with her.

"Come on. Please. Just this once to get him on my back."

"On your back? You mean *off* your back."

"That's what I meant. Please."

"No, sorry."

We came out of the woods. She turned to head to her house. I stopped and looked at her, waiting for a response. She paused.

"Have a good weekend," she said. Then she turned and walked away.

I had to do this by myself.

I turned for the park. It was early for our pickup game, so Malik and Blake were the only guys on the court shooting. I waved and walked up to the them. Maybe they could help.

"Blake, can you help me with something?" I asked.

"What do you need?" He passed me a basketball. I threw it at the hoop. It bounced off the backboard, hit the rim, and went the opposite direction.

"Hot spaghetti!" I jogged after the ball.

"Did you just say hot spaghetti?"

I nodded.

"You are a weird kid."

I shrugged.

"Caden won't leave me alone at school. Today he launched a football at me, and it hit me in the face." I heard a few chuckles from Malik. I ignored him. "I need it to stop."

"You have to stand up to the guy."

"How? You've seen him and me."

"You don't need to fight him. Fight him with words."

"What do you mean?"

"Find out something about him and use it against him."

"Like the girl he likes?"

Blake shot a three-pointer.

"Yes. That would work."

"I know that, but what do I do?"

"Does the school know that he likes her? Does she like him?"

"No and no."

He chuckled. "Perfect. Tell the whole school both of those things."

"That's it? But how?"

"I don't know. Just make sure he doesn't know that you did it."

"Why?"

"You just want to distract him from you, not make him even more angry at you."

"I don't know if I can do all that."

Blake passed me the ball. I took a shot from the free-throw line. The ball sailed into the hoop without touching the rim.

"Nice shot. Even if he does find out it's you, at least he will know that you aren't going to sit back and be pushed around by him."

"Oh, pug. This is going to be hard."

"Did you just say oh pug?"

"Yeah."

Blake shook his head.

"What?" I asked.

"Nothing. Let's play," he said with a laugh.

ELEVEN

I spent the weekend researching and devising the perfect plan to embarrass Caden. When I left for school Monday, I was ready. I cut a few flowers that had bloomed in our front yard and carefully placed them in my backpack.

I arrived at school with at least a half hour left before most students would be in the building. I taped all but one of the flowers to Maya's locker and then hurried to the locker room. I slid the remaining flower into Caden's gym locker and returned to the sixth-grade locker bay and waited.

Not long after, my classmates entered the building and the chatter of voices overtook the silence of the hallways. I stood down the hallway from my locker, waiting and watching. Students pointed at the flowers and whispered to each other.

When Maya arrived at her locker, she grabbed the flowers and opened her locker. She searched inside, but after a minute or two, she placed the flowers in her locker. She took her math book, slammed the locker shut, and walked away. She didn't have a big reaction, but I didn't expect her to.

I wandered the halls, listening to the students talking. Everybody in the sixth grade was talking about Maya's flowers and asking who liked her enough to give her flowers. I hadn't heard any names yet, but that was okay. Part one of the plan was complete, and everything was going according to the plan. I walked to class with an extra skip to my step.

When the bell rang for gym class, I took my time. For the first time since the start of the school year, I didn't want to be the first kid in the locker room. I waited until the second bell rang and then I went inside the locker room. When I opened the door, laughter was the first thing I heard. I swung the door open to see Caden and Jordan arguing.

"I didn't get her flowers, I swear," Caden said.

"Right," Jordan said. "Then why is there a flower in your locker?"

"I don't know!" Caden slammed his books down.

"You told me you thought she was cute, so you got her some flowers. Right?"

"No. I might have said that, but I wouldn't get her flowers." Caden turned his head and made eye contact with me. *Lickity split!* I dashed around the corner to my locker. I changed my clothes and got into the gym as fast as I could while I listened for Caden's voice. I heard the door slam shut. *He must have left the locker room.*

Some of the remaining boys started talking about Caden giving Maya flowers. I chuckled to myself. Part two was complete.

I left the locker room and entered the gym. I smiled at Maya, who was across the gym talking with a friend, but she ignored me. She probably hadn't noticed me. Mr. Wells entered the gym and started teaching us about football plays. I stayed in the back most of the football game, trying to keep out of Caden's way. He ignored me during the class and in the locker room. So far so good.

The tricky, final part of the plan began at lunch. Caden and Jordan placed their books and homework at a table, then got in the lunch line. I crept to the table and looked to the line. While they both had their backs to me, I fished through Caden's notebook and found an English assignment. I grabbed it, folded it, and placed it in my pocket. When I left the table, I noticed a few girls watching me. I smiled back and found an empty table in the back of the lunch room.

I opened the homework and looked at Caden's writing. It was surprisingly neat, which would make this easier. Using his homework as a guide, I wrote a note, copying his handwriting style. When I finished, the note definitely didn't look like I wrote it. I'm not sure the note looked like Caden wrote it either, but the signature was perfect.

I held on to the note until history, the last class of the day. My jitters led me to tap my foot on the floor and then my pencil on my desk. Midway through the class, Mrs. Roberts told me to stop because I was distracting the rest of the class. I stopped the jitters, but my heart felt like it was about to explode for the remainder of class.

When the final bell rang, I darted from my chair and followed Caden out the door. I stayed a few steps behind him, and when he arrived at his locker, I went for it. I tossed the folded-up note on the ground next to him and then darted behind the next locker bay. I peeked around it.

A sixth-grade girl named Lucy had the locker next to Caden's. She noticed the note on the ground and picked it up. I watched with anticipation as she unfolded the note and her eyes scanned the page. Her mouth slowly opened, then she shut her locker and skipped down the hallway to another girl's locker. Phase three of the plan was complete.

I strolled to my locker and packed up my homework for the night. Then I leaned against my locker and waited for Maya. A few minutes later, she hadn't arrived, so I went through the sixth-grade locker bay looking for her. I didn't see her anywhere, but I picked up on a few conversations of my classmates.

"He wrote her a love note!"

"Who does that these days?"

"What a dork!"

I chuckled when I heard those comments. I circled back to my locker, but Maya still wasn't there. I looked at the clock. Maybe she was with a teacher. I searched our sixth-grade classrooms, but no Maya. *I guess she was picked up from school today.*

I left the school without her and walked home alone. Even though Maya wasn't with me, I still took the path, hoping she had gone ahead, but the path was empty. *Oh pug.* I had a bad feeling in the pit of my stomach, but I didn't know exactly why.

I pushed through, going to the library and the park for my daily memory packing, half expecting to see Maya. I never saw her.

TWELVE

The next morning I woke up with a feeling of dread in the pit of my stomach, and I didn't know why. The Caden prank had gone as I planned, and I expected that he wouldn't bother me anymore. Or at least not any time soon. So why was I feeling bad? I left for school, but the cool, crisp autumn air added to the feeling that something wasn't right.

I arrived at school at the same time as the busses, so I followed the crowd inside. When I passed by Caden's locker, he didn't even look my way. I watched my sixth-grade classmates talking in groups and laughing, occasionally pointing at Caden. Everybody was talking about what happened yesterday.

Maya wasn't at her locker when I arrived, but I knew I would see her in math class. I grabbed my books and went to class. She didn't come in the classroom until seconds before the bell rang, so all I could do was say a quick hello. She didn't respond, but Mr. Makimoro was beginning his lesson.

When the lesson ended with about ten minutes left in class, I turned around in my seat.

"Hey," I said to Maya.

"Please don't talk to me," she replied and looked at her desk.

"What? Why?"

"You know why."

"No, I don't." I knew I shouldn't, but I focused in on her thoughts. *I can't believe you used me to get to Caden.* I wondered what she meant by used? As I tried to figure it out, the bell rang. I followed her into the hallway.

"We are done, Charlie. I can't believe you did that. Leave me alone." I could feel the emotion behind her words. She was upset, and I couldn't change her mind. I let her walk away while I stood frozen in the middle of the hallway with students passing on both sides.

———

Maya ignored me the rest of the day. Somehow the prank with Caden had upset Maya, but I didn't quite understand why. I knew she didn't want me to do it, but it seemed like more than simply not using my ability for good. I went through the motions of the school day, hoping for a chance to walk and talk with her after school. When the last bell rang, I jogged through the hallway to my locker.

"Maya," I said between breaths. "I don't know what I did, but I'm sorry."

"I know you don't understand the way everything works in middle school, but some things are universal. You don't use your friends so you can get ahead."

"What? Like ahead in line?"

"Oh my gosh. Talking to you is like talking to a kindergartner."

"I'm sorry?" I said.

"Just leave me alone. It's better this way. You don't have to worry about lying to your parents, and I don't have to deal with your weirdness."

"Maya, please." She shook her head and slammed her locker shut, leaving me alone.

I groaned and grabbed my backpack, and then left the school for the basketball court. Blake and Malik weren't there yet, so I sprawled on my back on the grass next to the court, staring into the sky. The fluffy, white clouds reminded me of a day on Europa when I was five years old. My parents had taken me to what is called a mountain on Earth. We went to the top where you could see far into the distance. I looked at the geyser pit on the bottom of the mountain. A fluffy, white mist surrounded a pit with streams of water of different colors that erupted every few minutes. It was one of the most beautiful things I have ever seen. I missed my home.

"Charlie, you all right?" Blake asked.

I blinked a few times and adjusted to the sunlight. For now, I was here, on Earth.

"Yeah, long day at school," I said, sitting up.

"Want to play?" he asked. I nodded, and he stretched his arm to help me up. Blake dribbled down the court and passed me the basketball. A few minutes later I had forgotten about all that happened that day. I knew enough basketball now that I didn't need to read anyone's mind. I just played.

"You're getting better," Malik said. Blake agreed.

"Thanks."

"Hey, Blake, I'm kind of stupid about things with friends. Can you explain something to me?"

"Okay."

I told him everything that had happened with Maya, Caden, and me minus the alien mind-reading part.

"You didn't just embarrass Caden. You embarrassed Maya."

"I did? How?"

"Nobody likes unwanted attention. Your school isn't just talking about Caden, now they are talking about Maya."

"But she didn't do anything."

"That doesn't matter. She's a part of all this."

"Lickity split. I really messed up. Didn't I?"

"Yeah."

"How do I make it up to her?"

"I don't know, man."

"Thanks anyway. I'll see you tomorrow."

I left the park and turned for home. The entire walk home I replayed everything that had happened over the past week. I thought about Caden and how he made me feel—insecure, small, and worthless. I thought about Maya and how I loved talking with her. I replayed the conversation where she told me not to mess with Caden. I didn't listen, and she didn't even know that I had her in part of my plans. With all these memories swirling in my head, I entered my house.

"Hello," my father said. He sat on the couch. I felt him enter my mind. "What's wrong?" he asked.

I didn't have time to react or to block my memories. He searched through the day.

"I messed up," I said, trying to stop him from going further. But he searched further. I felt him trying to understand it all.

"You've been keeping me out," he said. I looked to the ground.

"She knows," he added.

"I'm sorry, Dad. I didn't mean to tell her, but it came out, and then I didn't know what to do. I didn't want to move already. She's my friend. Or she was. I thought we could make it work."

"How long did you keep this from us?"

"Since the first week of school."

"Charlie, hiding isn't natural to us." He sighed. "I'm disappointed in you. You should have told me."

"I know. I didn't want to move."

"Son, you still need to be honest with us."

"I'm sorry."

"I'll tell your mother and sister. We'll figure out where to go next."

I felt a heaviness in my chest. Even with everything that had happened, I didn't want to move.

"Please, can't we stay?"

Dad shook his head. I felt a sadness and hurt in his heart. He didn't want to move either, but we didn't have a choice.

I plodded up the stairs and collapsed on my bed. Every part of me hurt. I wanted to fall asleep and start this week over.

THIRTEEN

My parents forced me to go to school the next morning. They knew I didn't want to go, so they drove me to school and watched me walk into the building. I thought about walking through the back door and leaving, but I didn't want to upset my parents further. Instead, I went through the school day in a daze, not paying attention to anything or anyone.

The final bell rang alongside a crack of thunder. I walked to the gym behind a few students. They opened the back doors and stopped. The rain was erupting from the skies.

"Man, the rain is coming down in cats and dogs," I said.

The brown-haired girl turned and looked at me.

"What are you talking about?" she asked.

Oh pug, I thought I got it right this time.

"The rain is really bad," I mumbled.

She shut the door and pulled out her cell phone. "Laura, can you pick me up?" she asked.

I opened the back door again. The rain seemed to fit my mood, so I stepped outside and started the walk home. My clothes were sopping after I'd walked five steps. No basketball today. Not that it mattered, but I would like to say good-bye to the guys. When I swung open our front door, I brought a puddle of water into the living room.

"Hey, why didn't you call me to come get you?" my mom asked. I shrugged. "How was your day?"

"Fine," I said. She entered my thoughts, and I didn't fight it as she searched through the day's memories.

"We are thinking about Chicago or Dallas. It would be a big change from our little town here in upstate New York, but Dad and I think we might blend in better in a big city."

"Makes sense," I mumbled. Then I squished my way upstairs to change out of my wet clothes.

———

The next day wasn't much different. Maya wasn't talking to me at school, so that meant nobody was talking to me at school. But at least Caden continued to ignore my presence instead of making my life any more miserable.

I spent the afternoon at home because of another rainy day, which kept me away from the basketball court. My parents hadn't told me of a decision about moving, but I didn't bother asking. They would tell me when they knew.

When I arrived at school Friday, Maya was at her locker. I didn't know for sure, but I figured it was my last day of school.

"Maya, can I talk to you for a minute?"

"No," she said.

"I'm leaving Silver Lake."

"Good." She turned and walked away.

Maybe moving was the right thing to do. Maybe I did need a new start.

After school, the sun burst through the clouds, drying the air from the rain of the past few days. I went to the park. I knew my parents wanted me to go home, but I had to see Blake and the guys one more time. They were at the court shooting, waiting for me.

"Hey, how did it go?"

"What go?"

"With the girl?"

"Not good. It doesn't matter anyway. I'm moving."

"You're moving? Didn't you just move here this summer?"

I nodded.

"Why?"

"It's hard to explain."

"Do you want to move?"

"Not really."

"Then fight it."

"It's not that simple."

"Sure it is. Tell your parents you aren't leaving. Tell the girl that you are sorry. Don't give up."

I looked at Blake. He had a toughness in his heart that I couldn't quite understand. I felt that it was genuine. He believed he could do anything if he tried, and he thought the same about me. That toughness and belief in yourself was something my family had once. We believed we could make it through anything, and we had by making it safely to Earth without being caught.

"You're right. I shouldn't give up yet. I will tell my parents that I don't want to leave."

"There ya go, fighter," Blake said.

"But in the end I have to follow them," I said.

"I get it. But you should at least tell them how you feel and try to change their minds."

"I don't know if I can ever change Maya's mind, even if I change my parents' minds."

"You've got us, too, Charlie," Blake said.

"Yeah, I do. You're right." I grabbed my book bag. "I need to go."

"See you tomorrow?" Blake asked.

"I hope so!"

I took off for my house. I ran all the way home,

with my book bag bouncing on my back. I burst through my front door. Katie was eating a snack at the table.

"Hi, Charlie," my mom said, entering from the kitchen.

"Mom, we need to stay here."

"We can't."

"Why?"

"You know why."

"Hear me out. Maya is the only person that knows. She won't tell anyone."

"You can't guarantee that."

"Yes, I can. Mom, we go to middle school. This isn't like school on Europa. She won't tell anyone because nobody will believe her, and they will think she is crazy. Trust me."

"He's right," Katie said. "People on Earth don't think aliens are real."

"We need to leave," my father said, entering the room. "It's not the people on Earth I'm worried about."

"Don't scare them," my mother said.

"They need to know the truth," my father said. "We aren't the only aliens on Earth."

"I know the other families are here, scattered across the planet."

"Yes, but there are rumors of other aliens living among us. Those are who I am worried about."

Fear crept into my heart. "From where?"

"We haven't figured that out yet."

I bit my lip.

"Until you do, can we stay? It doesn't make sense to move until we know more."

"True," my father said."

"Dad, I want to stay. I made some friends, and I'm starting to like basketball and get better at it."

My mother and father looked at each other.

"Maybe Charlie is right," Mom said. "We could give Silver Lake a chance for a little longer."

My father nodded. "Okay. But Charlie, you can't tell anyone else, and your friend can't tell anyone else. No more secrets."

"I promise. Thumb swear."

"Pinky swear," Katie said.

"Right. Pinky swear!" I raised my right pinky in the air.

"Then it's settled. We will stay," my father said.

I ran over to my parents. I gave my dad a high five, then my mom a low five, and joined hands. My sister ran over to us and squeezed in between my mom and dad. We stood in a circle and warmth radiated through our hands, and for the first time in a long time, I felt like everything was going to be okay. Then I remembered that my work wasn't over. I needed to get Maya to forgive me.

"Go," my dad said.

"I can't. Your hand is stuck to mine." My dad laughed and let my hand go.

I left the house and started down the street. Five minutes later, I turned around and went home.

"Dad, can I have twenty bucks?" I asked.

"For what?"

"I'm not sure yet."

He opened his wallet and handed me a twenty.

"Thanks."

I left the house again. This time I turned and headed in the direction of the town center. I needed to figure out a grand gesture to show Maya I wasn't a bad alien. Err. I mean guy.

FOURTEEN

As I wandered through the mall looking for the perfect gift for Maya, I realized that I didn't know much about her. We had spent all of our time talking about me and my problems. All I knew was that Maya was fast and athletic, so I focused on that one thing. I entered a shoe store.

All the shoes cost much more than the twenty-dollar bill, so I searched the shelves for the nicest pair of socks. I decided on a neon yellow pair because they reminded me of Maya. She always looked on the bright side of things. I paid for the socks and headed to the high school stadium for the football game.

I arrived a half hour before the game started, so the bleachers were empty. From my front row seat, I watched the football players stretching and throwing the ball. The school band sat in the bleachers next to the field. I stared at the sky, watching the yellow sun set in the horizon. The sun always looked red on Europa, and we only saw it for short periods of time. Europa was naturally dark, so the sun was closer to what people on Earth call stars or maybe the moon.

Although I missed my home, Earth was growing on me. It was beautiful in a whole new way. The people were the tough part. I couldn't quite understand the kids on Earth. Maya was the first person who I thought I understood. She had shown me that I could make this work.

While I watched the sun, the stadium began to fill with students, kids, and families. Most of the people were smiling and talking with each other. I stood and left the bleachers. I wandered to the gate, looking for Maya. Caden and Jordan walked in with a couple of other guys. They were laughing, but I didn't want to take any chance, so I hurried around the stadium, out of sight. I stopped at the concession stand.

"Popcorn, please," I asked.

"Two dollars."

"I'm out of money. Can I pay later?"

The man chuckled. "No."

I sighed. *Earth. No sense of trust.* I turned around, and I saw Maya's dark curls in the crowd.

Peaches and cream! I dashed through the crowd. She was walking with her two friends a few feet in front of me. I stopped, my heart beating faster. I didn't want to embarrass her.

I approached her. "Maya," I said. She flinched. "Can I talk to you for a minute?"

She turned around. "What do you want?"

"Can we talk? Please, it will only be a few minutes."

"Fine." She whispered something to her two friends, who looked at me and then walked ahead.

Maya and I walked to the fence bordering the football field.

"Well?"

"I convinced my parents to stay. I want to be here in Silver Lake. I want to be your friend. I want to help people."

She groaned and started to leave.

"Wait, Maya. I know that you have helped me so much already, but I know on Europa that being a friend is a three-way street."

"You mean two-way street." She smirked.

"Right. I mean I want to be there for you like you have been for me, so I got you these." I removed the gift from my coat pocket and handed it to her.

"Socks?"

"Not just any socks. The best socks at the mall for the fastest girl in the sixth grade." A big smile broke across her face.

"You bought me socks."

"Yes. Do you like them?"

"You are hopeless."

"I swear they are the best socks. Read the package about how they keep your feet cool for maximum performance."

"You are staying?"

I nodded.

"Your parents know about me?"

"Yes. I told them you would keep it a secret. Will you?" She nodded. "Maya, I'm sorry for what I did with Caden. I understand now how that hurt you. I didn't mean to do that."

"I know."

"You do?"

"Oh, yeah. You're too clueless to have done that on purpose. But I meant what I said about helping people, not hurting people with your ability."

"I know. You are right."

"Okay."

"Okay what?"

"I forgive you."

A smile broke across my face. I raised my hand up in the air.

"What are you doing?" she asked.

"High five!"

She shrugged and smacked my hand with hers.

"Awesome!"

"I need to get back to Sarah and Tiffany."

"Oh, yeah. Sure. My family is here somewhere. I need to find them so I can get some popcorn."

"We are sitting in the section by the band toward the top. Come say hi after you find your family."

"I will. Thanks, Maya."

She rejoined her friends. I stood at the fence as the buzzer sounded. The brown ball flew through the air, and the guys on the field ran toward each other, crashing into one another. I still didn't understand football, but maybe I would soon. I was sticking around. I smiled and wandered to the bleachers.

My family was crammed in the middle of a row near the top of the bleachers. My dad smiled and waved. I smiled back and took the steps two at a time up to them.

"How did it go?" my mother asked. "Never mind, I can tell from your smile. I don't even have to be in your head to know what happened."

"Yes. She promised to keep us quiet."

"You can go," he said.

"What?"

"I know you want to go sit with her."

"I didn't even notice you in my head."

"One day you will be as good as me, son." He winked.

"Can I have a few more dollars? I spent all of it on the socks."

"Socks?" all of them said in unison.

"I bought Maya socks." They squinted at me. I put out my hand. My dad gave me two dollars.

"That's only enough for one popcorn!"

"You said you wanted to fit in," my dad replied.

I groaned, swiped the two dollars, and skipped down the bleachers. I circled the stadium to the concession stand.

"One popcorn," I said.

"Do you have money?" the cashier asked. I gave him the two dollars.

"I told you I would pay you later." He laughed and turned around to the popcorn machine and grabbed two boxes. He handed me both boxes.

"The second one is my treat."

"Really?" He nodded. I took the boxes and left the booth. I downed both boxes of popcorn before I reached the band's side of the bleachers. Scanning the stands, I saw the trio of girls sitting by themselves near the top of the bleachers. Standing at the bottom of the bleachers, I waved. They didn't see me, so I trudged up the stairs.

"Hey," I said.

"Hi," Maya said. Tiffany giggled. *Why is everyone laughing at me tonight?* I sat at the end of the bleachers next to Maya.

"So, can any of you explain football to me?"

"You don't know football?" Sarah asked, leaning around Maya.

"No, they don't care much about football where I am from."

"Where are you from?"

"Cleveland," I said. My heart started to beat faster.

"I guess that makes sense," she said. "The Browns are terrible."

What are the Browns? I mumbled under my breath.

I watched the first half with the girls explaining the basics of what was happening in the game. At halftime, I accompanied the girls to the concession stand. They bought me a popcorn, and then I left to rejoin my family on the other end of the bleachers.

The second half had started, so only a few people were milling about under the bleachers. I felt the presence of two boys behind me. I focused in on their presence, and without looking at them I knew they were Caden and Jordan. I didn't have time to celebrate because my first instinct was to run. Something else inside me told me to face them, so I spun around.

"Hey, Caden and Jordan," I said.

"What do you want, loser?" Jordan asked.

"Nothing."

"Good. Go back and sit with your lame family," Caden sneered.

"I'm sitting with Maya," I blurted out.

"Yeah, right."

"No, I am. We are friends."

He started toward me. I backed up, running into the fence.

"What did you say?" I felt anger radiating from him. His face was inches away from mine. Maya's words echoed in my head. Use your power for good. Don't be like Caden. *Oh pug.* I didn't know what that meant when he was seconds away from knocking me in the nose.

"I'm sorry. I don't want any trouble."

"Leave him alone," Jordan said. "It's not worth it."

Caden backed away. "One of these days, I'm going to bash your face," he said.

"See you later," I said.

I scurried away from the fence back to my family in the bleachers. *Why did I just do that?* Now Caden would be bothering me again.

At least now I had Maya on my side.

FIFTEEN

Maya and I walked home Monday after a normal school day. I didn't go to the principal's office, get shoved in a locker, or do something stupid. It was a perfectly ordinary day on Earth. I loved it.

On the path, Maya turned to me. "Have you been reading my mind?"

"No," I said.

"But others?"

"Here and there," I said. "Sometimes it's by accident, but most of the time when I do it, I'm trying to learn something or practice the ability. If I don't practice, the ability can fade from me."

"I wish I could read my parents' minds." She looked at me. I shook my head. "I know. I'm not asking you to. It would just be nice to know what everyone is thinking."

"Sometimes I wish I didn't know. Especially here."

"What do you mean?"

"On Europa, most people were honest and transparent, so it didn't matter that we had this ability. We would tell each other the truth anyway."

"That's not the way it is here."

"Exactly."

"Then why did you leave? If everybody was so good on your moon?"

"A disease wiped out half of our population, and that allowed a bad group of people to take control of Europa. My family ran away so we wouldn't get captured for opposing their rule." I looked to the sky.

"I'm sorry."

"Me, too." I was glad she didn't ask any more questions. I didn't want to talk about it.

"I'm glad you found a safe place here in Silver Lake," she said.

"Me, too. See you tomorrow."

We parted ways. I turned for my house. The weather was nice, so I needed to change before meeting Blake and the guys at the basketball court. I picked up the pace without Maya by my side, but I felt someone close to me. I turned around, but I saw nobody. *Weird.* I kept walking. I turned into my driveway a few minutes later and entered my house, but that feeling still bugged me. I headed up the stairs and peeked out my window.

Caden.

He was staring at my house from across the street. Where did he come from? I focused on his mind and closed my eyes. I was in his head.

He set me up. Charlie Baker is going to pay for this. He turned and walked down the street.

Lickity split! Caden knew it was me.

———

When I reached the basketball court, the game was already underway.

"You're late," Malik said.

"Sorry, I had this thing."

"Jump in on my team," he said.

I ran to the basket on the first play, but I didn't look for the pass and the ball smacked me in the forehead. Stunned, I stood motionless for a minute. When I regained my bearings, the guys were already down the court. A few minutes later, Malik stopped the game.

"Your head isn't in the game. Everything okay?"

"Sorry, it's Caden again."

"He's still giving you a hard time?"

"Yeah, but I kind of deserve it."

"I doubt that."

"Ignore the guy."

"I've tried that."

"It's not working?"

"Nope," I said, "I'm at the beginning of my rope." *Wait, that didn't sound right.*

"You say weird stuff, Charlie."

"I mean the end of my rope," I whispered.

Blake passed me the ball. "You still want to play?" he asked.

"Yeah."

We played for another half hour. I didn't get hit in the head by the ball again, but I wasn't exactly on my game either. Not that I had much game. When I finished playing, I went to the library. Even if I didn't need the routine anymore, the habits were ingrained. I liked them.

———

I knew my dad was cooking because of the smell of burned meat combined with the haze in the air.

Yes. I am. The chicken is a little crispy on the edges, but it's edible.

I rounded the corner from the living room into the kitchen.

"Dad, I need your help," I said.

"What's wrong, son?"

I let him into the memories with Caden. "He's going to keep bullying me unless I do something. I know I shouldn't use my abilities on humans, but I don't know any other option."

"As long as you are using your ability to do the right thing, I don't see a reason why you can't use it."

"Really?"

"Yes."

"I'm not sure if my plan classifies as doing the right thing."

"Tell me."

I explained the plan to him.

"I see your dilemma. I think the key is to not hurt him or make fun of him in any way. That keeps your intentions pure."

"I hope Maya agrees."

"I think she will," my mother said. She stood in the entryway of the kitchen.

"Where did you come from? How did you ...?" I asked. "I didn't even feel your presence."

"I think some training is in order," my mom said. Then she smiled.

"Really?"

"Yes. Your father and I agree that it is best that you learn how to use your ability fully. You never know when you might need to use it."

"When does the training start?" I asked.

"Have you finished your homework?"

"Not yet."

"After you finish your homework, then."

"Peaches and cream!" I shouted. My parents laughed.

SIXTEEN

My parents dropped me off at school the next morning. They told me to wait, to let them train me a few more days, but I knew this was the day. If I didn't act today, I'd be stuck in a locker or garbage can by the end of the week.

I said hello to Maya at her locker, and when the bell rang, we walked to history together. I knew it was a risk not telling Maya about Caden, but I didn't want her in the middle of anything.

When the bell rang for gym class, I sprinted through the hallway to make it to the locker room first. I was in the gym with my gym clothes on before the second bell rang.

"Mr. Wells, what are we playing today?"

"Dodgeball." *Perfect.* Dodgeball was a game I understood. Don't get hit by the ball.

The rest of my classmates filtered into the gym. Caden and Jordan glared at me from across the floor while Mr. Wells explained the rules of dodgeball. When it was time to break into teams, I planted myself on the opposite team from Caden.

When the whistle blew, I stayed in the back to avoid any rogue balls until a blue foam ball rolled in front of me. I grabbed it, and then I focused in on Caden's mind. He was trying to hit Steve, another big athlete on my team. I waited for his focus to be completely on Steve and then launched the ball. I didn't have the best arm, but it was perfect. The ball sailed and hit him on the knees right after he released a ball toward Steve. I pumped my fists.

"Caden, you are out," Mr. Wells said.

Caden grimaced and moved out of the playing field with his eyes locked on mine. I smiled, and he glared at me.

Bonk. A ball hit me in my gut. I took my place in the back.

"What are you doing?" Maya asked.

"Playing the game."

"By hitting Caden? That's not a good idea."

"I've got this." I winked at her.

When the round ended, we all jumped back into the game. I knew I had to be extra careful now.

When the whistle blew, the game started again. This time Caden stayed back too. I took the first ball that came my way. Cautiously, I crept forward, but the balls were whizzing past me left and right. I backed up and let the competition settle. With only a few people left on both sides, I knew I had to make a move. I tuned into the minds of the four remaining players on the other team, including Caden.

My mom had given me a crash course on simultaneous mind reading the night before, and now I felt the weight of all of them in my mind. I waited for someone to lose focus on their surroundings. I threw the ball.

"You're out," Mr. Wells said to the guy I hit.

I picked off the next guy in the same way, leaving Jordan and Caden against me and Maya.

Maya?

We both moved out of range.

"You're still in."

"Of course. I'm the fastest girl in this school."

I laughed and looked down at her feet. "You are wearing the socks I got you!"

"They are nice socks," she said with a smile.

"I told you!" We laughed.

"What's your plan?" she asked.

"Win."

She sighed.

"When I say 'hot spaghetti,' throw the ball at Caden."

She chuckled and nodded.

We took several steps forward. Caden and Jordan did likewise. I tuned in and focused on them. They were both waiting. I needed to do something.

I sprinted forward, catching both of them off guard, and launched the ball at Jordan as both Caden and Jordan threw a ball at me.

"HOT SPAGHETTI!" I shouted as the world went into slow motion. One ball slammed against me in my chest, and the other hit me in the knees. *Oh pug, they both threw the ball hard.* As I crumpled to the ground, I watched the ball I threw graze Jordan's elbow and change course.

"Charlie and Jordan are out."

I looked at Caden, who was laughing at me, and so he didn't realize that a ball was zooming toward him. It hit him in the side.

"Caden is out. Maya wins!"

"Peaches and cream!" I shouted. "That was awesome!" I ran up to Maya and gave her a high five.

"Great throw," said Steve to Maya. A few other classmates congratulated Maya.

"Caden finally lost," said Mr. Wells. "Well played, Maya and Charlie." I turned to look at Caden. My mind was exhausted, but I didn't need to read his mind to know he wasn't mad. He was shocked that he'd lost to a girl.

———

By the end of the school day, the tale of the dodgeball game had spread beyond the sixth grade to the entire school. Maya was the star of the sixth grade. Everybody was talking about her and congratulating her for not only winning the game but also beating Caden. Not many of the students even knew I was in the same game as Maya and Caden.

Maya was at her locker surrounded by girls. I loaded my backpack and hurried around the bay to Caden's locker. Caden stood at his locker with slumped shoulders.

I can't believe I lost to a girl. At least it is Maya. If there is anyone to lose to, it's her. He shut his locker and walked away, alone. I didn't see Jordan anywhere. That was strange. I doubled back to my locker to find Maya alone, leaning against her locker, waiting for me.

"Hey," I said.

"Ready to go?" she asked. I nodded. When we crossed through the back doors, she stopped.

"Did you plan it?"

"Plan what?" I asked with a grin.

"To let me win in dodgeball."

"Not exactly. Your winning was much better than anything I dreamed up."

She laughed.

"I'm hoping Caden doesn't care about me at all anymore," I said.

"Do you think it worked?"

"I think so." She gave me a curious look.

"I know it has worked for now, but I don't know how long it will last," I said.

"You know, this is kind of what I meant when I said using your ability for good," she said.

"Using my ability to make you the star of the school?"

"No ..." She looked to the ground.

"I'm just kidding, you were already the star before I came."

She laughed. "I don't think so. This isn't about me. It's about doing good and making this school better for everyone, not just us."

"I don't know how else I can do good," I said.

"I have a few ideas."

"You do?" I asked. "Care to share?"

"Soon," she said. We stopped to take our separate paths home.

"Soon?" I asked.

"Yes, I need to formulate a better plan first." She smiled. "I'll see you tomorrow, friend."

"'Bye, Maya." I smiled and walked with a skip in my step the rest of the way home.

———

If you enjoyed this book, then you'll want to read Alien Kid 2: Goshen's Secret. I'll send you an ebook version for free if you leave a review of this book at your favorite online book store. Simply email me at kristen@kristenotte.com when the review goes live with the link or title of the review to receive Alien Kid 2 for free!

AFTERWORD

Thank you to my editor, Candace Johnson, for always fitting me into her schedule. Thanks to Glendon Haddix for his amazing cover design.

Thanks to my family and friends for not thinking I am crazy for writing kids' books about pugs and aliens.

Thanks to Lincoln for going to bed by 8pm so I have time to write!

Brian, I couldn't do this without your support. I love you.

John 14:12

ABOUT THE AUTHOR

Author Kristen Otte writes books for children, teens, and adults. She loves writing books that make kids laugh. Most of the time Kristen is chasing someone around her house–her son, her dogs, even her husband. If she isn't doing that, she is probably writing, reading, or enjoying the outdoors.

Learn more about Kristen and her books at
www.kristenotte.com
kristen@kristenotte.com

SERIES BY KRISTEN OTTE

The Adventures of Zelda is a laugh-out-loud chapter book series about a pug with an appetite for adventure.

- The Adventures of Zelda: A Pug Tale
- The Adventures of Zelda: The Second Saga
- The Adventures of Zelda: Pug and Peach
- The Adventures of Zelda: The Four Seasons
- The Adventures of Zelda: The One & Only Pug

What happens when a mind-reading alien goes to middle school? *Alien Kid* is an exciting, new middle grade series.

- Alien Kid
- Alien Kid 2: Goshen's Secret
- Alien Kid 3: The Principal Problem

Eastbrook is a contemporary young adult series focused on teenagers trying to find their way with family, friends, and sports for ages 13 and up.

- The Perfect Smile (Eastbrook 0.5)

Made in the USA
Middletown, DE
16 July 2019